AMANDA PIG
AND HER BIG
BROTHER OLIVER

Jean Van Leeuwen
PICTURES BY
ANN SCHWENINGER

DIAL BOOKS FOR YOUNG READERS

NEW YORK

Dial easy-to-read

Published by
Dial Books for Young Readers
2 Park Avenue
New York, New York 10016
Published simultaneously in Canada
by Fitzhenry & Whiteside Limited, Toronto
Text copyright © 1982 by Jean Van Leeuwen
Pictures copyright © 1982 by Ann Schweninger
Printed in Hong Kong by South China Printing Co.
COBE
2 4 6 8 10 9 7 5 3
The Dial Easy-to-Read logo is a trademark of
Dial Books for Young Readers,
a division of E. P. Dutton, a division of New American Library,
® TM 1,162,718

Library of Congress Cataloging in Publication Data
Van Leeuwen, Jean. Amanda Pig and her big brother Oliver.
Summary: Presents five stories about telling secrets,
playing alone, and other activities in the lives of
Oliver and Amanda, who are sometimes known as Mighty Pig
and Amazing Baby Pig.
[1. Pigs—Fiction. 2. Brothers and sisters—Fiction]
I. Schweninger, Ann, ill.   II. Title.
PZ7.V3273Am [E] 82-1557 AACR2
ISBN 0-8037-0016-4
ISBN 0-8037-0017-2 (lib. bdg.)

The art for each picture consists of a pencil and wash drawing
with two halftone color separations.

Reading Level 1.8

For David and Elizabeth,
the Oliver and Amanda
I used to know

J. V. L.

To Uncle Quenty and Aunt Betty

A. S.

CONTENTS

THE BEST TRICK

"Watch me, Father," said Oliver.

"I am watching," said Father.

"This is my fastest run,"
said Oliver.

Oliver ran very fast
to the apple tree
and very fast back.

"My," said Father.

"That certainly was a fast run."

"Me too," said Amanda.

Amanda ran very fast

to the apple tree.

But she tripped on her feet

and fell smack on her ear.

"This is my biggest jump,"
said Oliver.
Oliver climbed up on a rock
and jumped very far.

"My," said Father.
"That certainly was a big jump."

"Me too," said Amanda.

Amanda climbed up on a rock

and jumped very far.

But her feet got tangled up,

and she fell smack on her bottom.

"This is my highest throw,"
said Oliver.
Oliver threw his ball
very high up in the sky.

"My," said Father.
"That certainly was a high throw."
"Me too," said Amanda.
Amanda threw her ball
very high up in the sky.

But it came right down again
and bounced on her head.

She fell smack on her nose.
Amanda began to cry.
Father picked her up
and kissed where it hurt.

"My oh my oh my," he said.

"Oliver has a lot of good tricks.

He can run and jump

and throw a ball very well.

But Amanda is the best

at falling down

of anyone I know.

Can you do it again?"

Amanda stopped crying.

She fell down again.

And again.

And again.

"Amazing," said Father.

"Not bad," said Oliver.

Amanda laughed.

She fell down again,

smack on her stomach.

THE SECRET

It was raining outside.

Inside, Mother and Oliver and Amanda
were sitting in the big chair,
having a hug.

"Tell me a secret," said Oliver.

"All right," said Mother.

Mother whispered a secret
into Oliver's ear:
"We are as snug
as three bugs in a rug."

"Me too," said Amanda.

"First I have to tell my tiger," said Oliver.

Oliver whispered the secret into his tiger's ear:

"Three bugs are having a hug."

"Now me," said Amanda.

Oliver's tiger whispered the secret into Amanda's ear:

"Three bugs are on the rug."

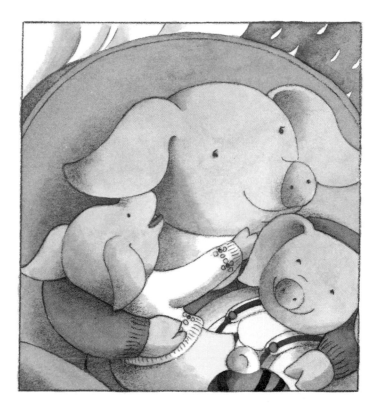

"Can you tell me, Amanda?"

asked Mother.

Amanda whispered the secret

into Mother's ear:

"Bug in your ear."

"What bug?" cried Mother. "Where?"
Mother jumped up and

turned around

and slapped the air

and slapped her ear.

Oliver and Amanda

fell in a heap on the floor.

Mother fell on top of them.

"Oh, dear," said Mother.

She sat up.

"Where did the bug go?" she asked.

"There was no bug," said Oliver.

"It was just a secret."

Mother laughed.

Oliver and Amanda laughed.

They laughed and laughed.

"That was a silly secret,"

said Mother.

And the three of them

had another big hug

on the rug.

ME TOO

"This is my magic cape,"
said Oliver.
"With my magic cape I can fly
through the air like a bird."

"Me too," said Amanda.

Oliver flew through the air

like a bird.

But he bumped into Amanda.

"Go away, Amanda," said Oliver.

"These are my magic boots.
With my magic boots I can leap
over tall buildings."
"Me too," said Amanda.
Oliver leaped over a tall building.
But he tripped over Amanda.

"Stop copying me, Amanda,"
said Oliver.

"And now for my greatest trick."

"Me too," said Amanda.

"I can't do it," said Oliver.

"You're standing on my cape."

"Sorry," said Amanda.

Oliver flew through the air

and leaped over a tall building

and saved his tiger

from the bad guys.

But he landed on top of Amanda.
The tall building fell down
and the bad guys got away.

"I give up," said Oliver.

"Amanda, you are always in my way.

I'm going to have lunch."

"Me too," said Amanda.

"I'll have a peanut butter

and banana sandwich

with two slices of bread

and an orange and a cookie

and a glass of milk," said Oliver.

"My, you must be hungry,"
said Father.

"I am Mighty Pig, the strongest pig
in the world," said Oliver.

"Me too," said Amanda.

"There's only one Mighty Pig," said Oliver. "And I'm it."

"I want to be Mighty Pig too," said Amanda.

"Father," said Oliver, "why does Amanda do everything I do?"

"Because I am little," said Amanda.

"Amanda is little now," said Father.
"But she wants to be big like you.
Do you think you can help her
learn to be big?"
Oliver took a big bite of his
peanut butter and banana sandwich.

"Well," he said,
"I could show her how to lift
a tall building with one hand.
And how to scare away monsters
just by looking at them."

"That is a good idea," said Father.

"But she can't be Mighty Pig,"

said Oliver.

"She can be the Amazing Baby Pig."

"Okay," said Amanda.

"Watch this," said Oliver.

"Mighty Pig will now eat

a whole cookie in a single bite."

"Me too," said Amanda.

THE BAD GUYS

"Uh-oh," said Oliver.

"They're out there."

"Who is out there?" asked Amanda.

"The bad guys," said Oliver.

"This looks like a job

for Mighty Pig."

"Me too?" said Amanda.

"Okay," said Oliver.

"But the Amazing Baby Pig

has to do whatever Mighty Pig says."

Oliver got out his zoom-mobile.

"I drive," he said.

"You push."

Oliver drove to the apple tree.

"This will be our fort," he said.

"You get some rocks and build a wall
and get some sticks and build a fort
and then make a hundred mudballs.
I'll watch out for bad guys."

Oliver came down from the tree.
"The bad guys are over there,"
he said. "I'm going after them.
You stay here and guard the fort."
Oliver went after the bad guys.
He knocked them out
and tied them up
and dragged them back to the fort.

"That will teach those bad guys,"
he said. "We're taking them to jail.
I drive. You push."

"No," said Amanda.

"What did you say?" asked Oliver.

"No!" said Amanda.

"You can't say no," said Oliver.

"I am Mighty Pig.
You have to do what I say."

"No no no no no!" shouted Amanda.

She threw a mudball at Oliver.

Oliver threw a mudball back.

They both went to the kitchen.

"Oliver and Amanda," said Mother.

"You are covered with mud."

"Amanda threw a mudball at me,"

said Oliver.

"She is no fun.

All she says is no."

"Well," said Mother,

"you will both have to take a bath."

"No!" said Amanda.

"See what I mean?" said Oliver.

"I see what you mean," said Mother.

"But I bet you can get Amanda

to say yes."

"I can?" said Oliver.

Mother ran the water in the bathtub.

"Come on, Amanda," said Oliver.

"We have to take a bath."

"No!" said Amanda.

"Please?" said Oliver.

"No!" said Amanda.

"I have an idea," said Oliver.

He went to the bathtub and put in

all of Amanda's favorite things:

her whale and her teacups

and her ball with the fish inside

and a lot of bubblebath.

"Look, Amanda," he said.

"We can put bubbles in the cups

and play tea party."

"No," said Amanda.

"And we can pretend

we are fish swimming," said Oliver.

"No," said Amanda.

"And I will let you sail

my new boat," said Oliver.

"Yes," said Amanda.

Mother smiled.

"You did it, Oliver," she said.

"Come on, Amazing Baby Pig,"
said Oliver.

"Let's swim."

ALL BY HERSELF

"Today," said Oliver,

"I want to do something with Father.

Just the two of us."

"What would you like to do?"

asked Father.

"Play checkers," said Oliver.

"Me too," said Amanda.

"Not you too today," said Father.

"Today Oliver and I

are playing checkers.

Just the two of us."

Amanda watched Father and Oliver

set up the checkerboard.

"What would you like to do today?"
asked Mother.

"Play with Oliver," said Amanda.

"Oliver is busy right now,"
said Mother.

"Play with you," said Amanda.

"I am busy too," said Mother.

"You will have to play by yourself
for a little while."

"I can't," said Amanda.

"I'm too little."

"Why don't you go to your room,"
said Mother,

"and see if you can find a toy
to play with all by yourself?"

Amanda went to her room.

She looked at all her toys.

She didn't see anything

that she could play with

all by herself.

She sat down on the floor.

"Ouch," she said.

She was sitting on

one of Oliver's blocks.

Amanda looked at it.

She stood it on end.

"That is a door," she said.

She put another block on top.

"That is a window," she said.

She got some more blocks.

"That is a wall and that is a roof

and that is a chimney on top.

Look, Mother," she called.

"I made a house."

Mother came to see.

"What a fine big house," she said.

"I'm going to make it bigger,"
said Amanda.

She got some more blocks.

"That is a very high wall

and that is a tower

and that is a flag place on top.

Look, Mother," she called.

"I made a castle."

Mother came to see.

"What a fine big castle," she said.

"We finished our game," said Father.

"Come see the castle

that Amanda made

all by herself," said Mother.

Father and Oliver came to see.

"Super-duper," said Father.

"Not bad," said Oliver.

"Come on, Amanda.

Let's go outside

and play Mighty Pig

and the Amazing Baby Pig."

"No," said Amanda.

"No?" said Oliver.

"No," said Amanda.

"I am busy right now."

She got the rest of the blocks
from the closet.

"Now I am going to build a city,"
she said.

"All by myself."